I0847371

PRAISE

"Mary Davis offers an invaluable resource for long-distance caregivers. Her compassionate guidance and practical tips make navigating the complexities of caregiving from afar manageable and effective. This book is a must-read for anyone looking to provide the best care for their loved ones, regardless of distance. Davis' expertise and heartfelt advice truly shine through every page."

Dr. Jane Thompson, Geriatric Specialist

"In *Making a Difference: Caregiving From Afar,* Mary Davis masterfully addresses the unique challenges faced by remote caregivers. Her insightful strategies and real-life examples offer hope and practical solutions to those struggling with the emotional and logistical aspects of caregiving from a distance. This book is an essential tool for modern caregivers striving to balance their responsibilities and provide quality care. Davis' empathetic approach and deep understanding of the subject make this a standout guide."

Rebecca Lawson, Executive Director of
Caregiver Support Network

"Mary Davis' book is a comprehensive and heartfelt guide for anyone providing care from a distance. Her clear, concise advice covers every aspect of long-distance caregiving, from communication to crisis management. *Making a Difference: Caregiving From Afar* is an essential addition to any caregiver's library, filled with practical tips and emotional support. Davis' dedication to helping caregivers is evident in every chapter."

Michael Anderson, Author of
The Caregiver's Companion

"Through *Caregiving from Afar,* Dr. Mary Davis provides authentic and heartwarming stories of family challenges with recommendations of relevant and timely resources."

Dr. Deidre Houston Magee, Family
Caregiving Expert/Coach

MAKING A *Difference*
CAREGIVING FROM AFAR

MAKING A *Difference*
CAREGIVING
FROM AFAR

Mary McGlothin Davis, PhD, RN

mcglothin davis INC.

McGlothin Davis, Inc.
Denver, Colorado

To the caregivers, who took the time and heartfelt energy to tell the inspiring stories that will benefit countless others who will take on the role of caregivers from afar in the future.

To my dear daughters, Dianna and Caryn, who held my hand with encouraging words and assistance as I took on the task of making this book a reality.

To my other family members, who have helped to make my caregiving story a reality throughout my lifetime.

To friends, who encouraged me through the years whenever I've told them my vision of making Making Difference: Caregiving from Afar *a reality, even with what may have appeared to some to be "pie in the sky" thinking.*

CONTENTS

Preface xiii

1. Aunt Clea: My Family Caregiving Story 1

2. Nuna's Story 13

3. Leila's First-Person Caregiving Account 21

4. Tangela's Experience 31

5. Francis' Long Distance Caregiving 43

6. Alexandria's Story 57

7. Neva's Caregiving 67

8. Sarah's First-person Caregiving Account 79

9. Mae's Caregiving Experience 87

10. Andre's Caregiving Story 99

11. From Caregiving Surveys to Caregiving
Stories 109

Final Thoughts on Caregiving Action Planning ... 137

Caregiving from Afar Resource List 151

About the Author 155

PREFACE

My name is Mary. During my life, I've been called daughter, Mom, Grandma, Auntie, Little Sister, Big Sister, Cousin, Neighbor, and Friend. Most importantly, for 51 years I was Don's wife. In all of these roles, I experienced family with all of its complexities. I was loved, nurtured, and cared for by my parents, grandparents, and siblings. I fulfilled those same roles during my marriage. As the years passed, I served as caregiver for my parents, in-laws, husband and aunt. From my life's journey, I recognize the natural progression of individual growth and independence. Many people list their independence among the things that are most important to them. Even small children are proud of the day that they learn to tie their shoelaces, teenagers enjoy the freedom that comes with earning their driver's license, and senior adults seek to retain their driving privileges and other forms of independence for as long as possible.

Unfortunately, as we age, we sometimes have to fight to remain independent. Those who are caring for an aging loved one are likely familiar with this power struggle. It can take some creativity and gentle persuasion to help a loved one remain safe, maintain their independence, and age gracefully at home.

It is estimated that more than 7 million Americans provide or manage care for someone age 55 or older who lives at least an hour away. Long-distance caregivers may feel guilty and anxious because they often can't be there to see how the loved one is doing and may feel overwhelmed by the challenges of arranging services from afar.

But former first lady Rosalyn Carter reminded us in *Helping Yourself Help Others:* "There are only four kinds of people in the world – Those who have been caregivers. Those who are currently caregivers. Those who will be caregivers. And those who need caregivers."

This book shares a combination of first-person accounts and interviews from long distance caregivers. These caregivers, although from different backgrounds, traversed often unfamiliar territory of caregiving for a loved one. As you read their stories imagine hearing their voices. While reading and listening, you may identify with similarities you, your family or friends have experienced, are encountering or expect to face in the near future. The stories are those of ordinary people who encountered extraordinary or unexpected circumstances. Each is presented in brief, yet powerful voices, with the names of all contributors kept anonymous except mine (i.e., the author). They were enthusiastic in speaking about their experiences and in some cases appeared relieved to share their caregiving tales.

Each story ends with a highlight of lessons learned by the person who was honored to share the gift of caregiving with their loved one. In addition, where possible, a summary of a best practice highlighted in the story is noted. One best practice is a take-off of the "It takes a village" mantra, from the title of Hillary Clinton's best-selling book, *It Takes a Village to Raise a Child*. In the case of an adult family member, often a supportive, nurturing community, "village," is needed to stay as healthy and safe as possible during their senior years.

Another best practice cited is to check in regularly. Several stories include accounts of how checking in regularly was a consistent practice. This included consistent reassurance for the care receiver and the caregiver. These were not always lengthy check-ins, but essential ones. Visits that are too far apart also open the possibility of more serious situations going unaddressed, such as a fall, injury, urgent home repair, or spills on the floor, etc.

Storytellers also spoke about the importance of building and maintaining a network of neighbors or other informal caregivers who can be trusted to check in or visit the loved one as needed. A simple request for help while providing neighbors or other trusted informal caregivers with contact information, can prevent a potentially dangerous situation that may go unnoticed otherwise. It can be surprising how much some people, including long-time associates including church members, are willing to help.

So, as you go through the stories, you will discover easy to implement strategies for caring for a loved one from afar. The accounts are refreshing, and, in most cases, the caregiving practices are easy to put into place.

At the end of each story, you will find Notes pages to write your own caregiving thoughts.

MAKING A DIFFERENCE: CAREGIVING FROM AFAR

Aunt Clea and Me

AUNT CLEA: MY FAMILY CAREGIVING STORY

"With Mama's passing, the seven of us felt responsible for Aunt Clea's well-being, financially and personally."

When we were children, we always looked forward to going to Aunt Clea's and Uncle Charlie's house. Aunt Clea and Uncle Charlie lived "in town" whereas we lived in the country, eight miles from the city limits of our small town in northeast Texas. Mama and Daddy had seven children. Aunt Clea and Uncle Charlie had none. We looked up to them as our well-to-do relatives who lived in a nice white house with a long driveway and a garage to park their car inside. As a child, I remember going to Aunt Clea's office at Atlanta Life Insurance Company. I admired her status as a professional who wore fancy navy-blue suits. Uncle Charlie was a pull-man porter who worked at a major railroad company. They were our role models of what we considered successful professionals.

Our parents took very good care of us, ensuring we had all of our basic needs met. Daddy managed his own auto repair business next to our house and was respected as "Mr. Penny," the community mechanic. Mama always wanted to have a paying job so she could have "nice things" like Aunt Clea, but Daddy gently insisted that she already had a job – being his partner raising the seven of us. When Uncle Charlie passed away in 1990, Mama was already living in their home. Daddy had died in 1975, at which time Uncle Charlie and Aunt Clea invited her to live with them. She did so until she passed away in 1994. With Uncle Charlie's passing, the company he worked for terminated his retirement pension. This left Aunt Clea with very limited financial resources, solely her small Social Security Retirement Pension. Mama could provide very little assistance because her only income had come from Daddy's small Social Security Retirement pension.

With Mama's passing, the seven of us felt responsible for Aunt Clea's well-being, financially and personally. In my case, I began to send a monthly check to my eldest sister, who lived in our hometown, and was Aunt Clea's primary caregiver, to ease the burden of taking care of her financial needs.

In early 2000, at age 83, Aunt Clea suffered disabling stroke, leaving her paralyzed on one side of her body, and unable to walk. So basically, she was for the most part bedridden except for the caregiving assistance given by two of my sisters who lived in our hometown. In later years, she was able to secure the assistance of part-time in-home caregivers funded by Medicaid. My challenge: Being 1,200 miles away I was limited in how I could participate in Aunt Clea's care. Early on I gave a lot of thought to how I could make a difference in helping Aunt Clea stay in good spirits and as independent as possible.

I continued to send my oldest sister six months of personal checks at a time to use for Aunt Clea, in whatever ways she felt was best. She told me later that she used the money each month for Aunt Clea's beauty shop appointments. That made me feel good because Aunt Clea was always so proud of her appearance. This way I could be a part of her maintaining her self-esteem. Because I had a toll-free number connected to my business, I sent Aunt Clea a stick-on label that included the number to attach to her phone. This way she could call me whenever she desired, at no cost. The phone calls helped us stay connected over the years. I ordered cut flower arrangements that were delivered to Aunt Clea's home by a local florist each holiday and on her birthday. It was not until she told me I was the only one who sent her cut flowers that I realized that I was truly a part of her caregiving team – making a difference with my one-of-a-kind contributions.

This experience taught me a number of lessons, about myself as well as how I could be a long-distance caregiver. I learned I could do simple things that others had not thought about but could make a positive difference. I've also learned to be patient with myself, recognizing my limitations, and at the same time I've become aware of my unique caregiving contributions. I have also become adept as being a sounding board for others who may be in similar situations. While I don't expect others to follow the same path, I've let them know they can show their love in their own way. For sure, it's never too late to start on a satisfying caregiving journey.

Aunt Clea lived in a local nursing home the last four years of her life, until she passed on at 102 years old. Aunt Clea remained in good spirits throughout this period and looked forward to receiving her cut flowers, and our telephone conversations. In the summer of her 100th birthday,

I was one of the planners for her centennial celebration. By fulfilling this role, I was able to energize others – especially younger family members to become part of her ongoing caregiving. In addition, I modeled how they could provide care for other family members as we all age.

A Time for Reflection

"Being a family means you are a part of something very wonderful. It means you will love and be loved for the rest of your life."
— Lisa Weed (veeroesquotes.com)

Lessons Learned from Caring for Aunt Clea from Across the Miles

Over the past two years, I've had the opportunity to reflect on the following words of wisdom a fellow "Outward Bound Retreat" colleague shared during one of our team building sessions: "What is given does not end." I've reflected on what Aunt Clea gave to me secretly such as keepsake silverware and other things, about which she implored me to not tell anyone else.

One everlasting gift she shared before suffering the stroke was the handwritten recipe she titled "Aunt Clea's Peanut Clusters," which is a luscious candy recipe that my immediate family has enjoyed; and now I get to share with anyone reading this caregiving account. It is indeed a "never ending gift."

Aunt Clea's Peanut Clusters Recipe

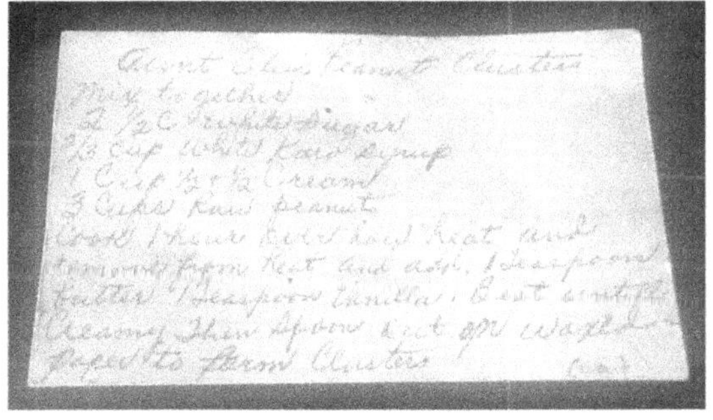

On the other side of the card is

"Add 1/4 Teaspoon Salt"

<u>Recipe repeated</u>
Mix together:
2 ½ C White Sugar
2/3 Cup White Karo Syrup
1 Cup ½ & ½ Cream (*half and half Cream*)
3 Cups Raw Peanuts

Cook 1 hour over low heat (*suggest 275-300 degrees*) and remove from heat and add 1 Teaspoon Butter and 1 Teaspoon Vanilla. Beat until Creamy, then spoon out on waxed paper to form clusters.

Suggested Actions

Many people are aging who were childless or their children have passed or are unable to care for them, therefore:

- This is a time you may feel your calling is to help an extended family member, whether it is an aunt, uncle, cousin or godparent.

- It's a good idea to write down your memories of these family members' contributions with your upbringing.
- By doing so, such a list can remind both you and your loved one being cared for why you chose to care for them as they cared for you during your youth.
- Taking time to reminisce with your loved one about what you can remember about happy times can make both of you smile and feel happy, thereby contributing to their well-being.

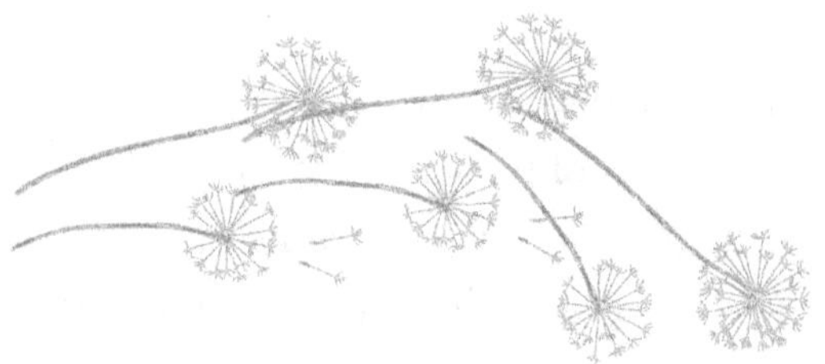

Chapter 1 Summary

- ❏ Do simple things that others haven't thought about that make a positive difference.

- ❏ Be patient with yourself.

- ❏ Become aware of your unique caregiving contributions.

- ❏ Recognize personal limitations.

- ❏ Show love in your own way.

- ❏ Become a sounding board for others who are in similar situations.

- ❏ It's never too late to start on your own caregiving journey.

Notes

Notes

NUNA'S STORY

"Each time the two daughters offered to come, their mom's husband assured them he could handle all of their mother's care by himself. He actually discouraged them from making the journeys. This reassurance was not reassuring at all, but Nuna and her sister did not want to intrude on the stepfather's and their mother's space."

For many years, Nuna who lived 2,000 miles away from her mother and stepfather, had a feeling that all was not well with her mother's health and well-being. At age 87, their mother, a published author and accomplished artist, was in and out of hospitals and other healthcare facilities for treatment of a variety of serious health issues. At that point, Nuna and her younger sister asked their stepfather if they could come to assist with their mother's care. Even though their stepfather had never been welcoming of Nuna and her sister in his and their mother's home over the four plus decades of marriage, the daughters thought he might appreciate having a break in their mother's day-to-day caregiving tasks. Each time the two daughters offered to come; their mom's husband assured them he could handle all of their mother's care by himself. He actually discouraged them from making the journeys. This reassurance was not reassuring at all, but Nuna and her sister did not want to intrude on their stepfather's and their mother's space. This was, in part, their sense that he had been very controlling of their mother and how much she shared with her daughters throughout the marriage.

After so many efforts to find out what was going on, Nuna's sister, who lived 2,500 miles away, scheduled a visit to check on their mom. When her sister arrived at their mother's and stepfather's home, she found her mother was in a rehabilitation center. Their mother was in the facility for radiation and chemotherapy treatment for an advanced cancer diagnosis. As soon as her sister arrived at their mother's bedside, she called Nuna and told her to come right away. Nuna made the trip immediately and upon arrival contacted the medical team responsible for their mother's care. Nuna was shocked when the lead physician told her and her sister their mom was at the end-of-life and needed hospice care. Needless to say, Nuna and her sister then felt their stepfather was likely in denial of the seriousness of their mother's condition or felt it was none of Nuna's and her sister's business. Either way, they saw their stepfather's actions in this instance being reflective of his ongoing controlling behavior he had exhibited toward their mother.

Nuna immediately arranged for in-home hospice care, became her mother's primary caregiver and stayed at her mother's bedside in the next several weeks until she passed away peacefully.

Suggested Actions

While this is not the typical long distance caregiving account, for Nuna it reflects the need for loved ones living far away to be persistent and insistent in asking and getting answers to the right questions. In other words, when you feel you are not getting the full story of what is going on when it comes to the health and well-being of a loved one, press on until you can receive the full story.

Following is the Chapter 2 Summary with some questions to enhance communications in caregiving situations.

Chapter 2 Summary

- ☐ Ask to speak to your loved one.

- ☐ What is their primary diagnosis?

- ☐ What is their daily routine?

- ☐ What kind of activities of daily living do they need assistance with?

- ☐ What is their daily food intake?

- ☐ Are there any foods they would prefer?

- ☐ What medications or other treatments have been prescribed? How often?

- ☐ How often is your loved one taking the medication and/or other treatment?

- ❑ What is the name, specialty, and contact information of their primary healthcare practitioner?

- ❑ When was the last time they visited their physician or healthcare practitioner?

- ❑ If your loved one is in a care facility, what is the address and how long have they been in the facility?

"Home was the place for me, and I never wanted to leave it. I would go for visits only when Grandmother was with me."

Quote from memoir written and published by Nuna's mom.

Notes

Notes

3.

LEILA'S FIRST-PERSON CAREGIVING ACCOUNT

"We have also developed a new appreciation for how important it is to be there for the caregiver, and to provide physical, spiritual, and moral support, not just for the "patient" but for the caregiver as well."

My mother (Momma) lived about a mile away from my sister, Elka. She moved there after my father's death. All four of us siblings agreed that Momma should move close to one of us, so she would have someone nearby. Momma chose Elka's hometown, in part because she was least likely to move. (Momma was right, because three of us moved to other states.)

For many years things went well with this arrangement. Elka enjoyed having Momma nearby, and Momma loved being close to Elka and her grandchildren. As she aged, it became apparent that Momma was losing her mental faculties, and it was agreed that she should move into Elka's house, because she should not be alone. Elka hired a caregiver, but felt the pressure of being responsible for our mother. She refused to explore the option of a home for the elderly; meanwhile Momma's dementia became more and more severe. She lost the ability to talk or communicate, and even physically seemed to have diminished a little each time I saw her.

Over the years, I tried to be there when she needed me, but it was clearly not enough. Elka felt totally abandoned. By the time Momma died, Elka was angry with all of us. It wasn't until well after the funeral, as my other sister and I tried to debrief what had happened, that we realized that while everyone was concerned about how Momma was doing,-- was she suffering? Did she need anything? Could we do anything for her? No one was focusing on Elka's needs. None of us acknowledged the burden that all this was placing on her. We totally dropped the ball, and it was bouncing up and down – squarely on Elka's shoulders.

My siblings and I have had many talks and have reconciled. We have also developed a new appreciation for how important it is to be there for the caregiver, provide physical, spiritual, and moral support, not just for the "patient" but for the caregiver as well. It's tough to be the caregiver. I and all of my siblings need to make sure that we appreciate and value what those caregivers provide.

Action: Who Takes Care of the Caregiver?

It is not unusual that one person takes on the responsibility of being the primary caregiver. Depending on family dynamics, there may be an expectation that one person naturally fits that role. While this may be true, leaving the total or near total responsibility on this person can result in unexpressed tension and downright anger. This person may feel that other family members "should" know they need help or that they need a respite from the day-to-day caregiving. Open family communication about caregiving needs of a loved one, early in the caregiving cycle, is an important strategy to a balanced and healthy caregiving journey.

- One approach is for the family members from afar to conduct a caregiving audit, a review of how well the loved one is able to complete what are commonly known of activities of daily living independently, in a timely way and safe manner.
- Some people use a visit, during holidays, or other nonintrusive times, to conduct the safety audit.
  - Activities of daily living include tasks, at a minimum, personal hygiene – bathing/showering, grooming, nail care, and oral care; dressing – being able to make

appropriate clothing decisions and physically dress and undress oneself.
- ○ Other aspects to be assessed include the loved one's ability to handle financial matters, take medications with or without assistance, as well as possible personality or mobility changes.

For families who find themselves in a similar situation, either from the caregiver perspective or that of other siblings or other close family members, there are some time-tested resources for preventing hurt feelings.

Resources offered online by the nationwide nonprofit organization, AARP include *5 Tips for Difficult Caregiving Conversations* are summarized below:

- Talk early and often.
- Observe and do your homework before acting.
- Communicate effectively.
- Include key people in the conversation.

- Approach with love, concern and support, remembering that all have a single goal: the best possible care and quality of life for your loved one. This and other resources can be found online at AARP.org/caregiving.

Chapter 3 Summary

- ❑ Family Members from Afar Can Conduct a Caregiving Audit: A review of how well the loved one can perform everyday activities

- ❑ Other Aspects to assess is the loved one's abilities to handle financial matters, take medication, possible personality or mobility change

- ❑ AARP also recommends:

    1. Talk early and often.

    2. Observe and do your homework before acting.

    3. Communicate effectively.

    4. Include key people in the conversation.

5. Approach with love, concern, and support, remembering that everyone has a single goal: the best possible care and quality of life for your loved one.

Notes

Notes

9.

TANGELA'S EXPERIENCE

"Sadly, I learned that not everyone sees or handles their responsibilities at the same level. I had expectations of how family members who lived closer would participate in my grandmother's care. That did not manifest, which led to feelings of resentment."

Tangela feels honored to have provided caregiving for her grandmother who lived approximately 1,800 miles away, on the opposite coast of the United States. As Tangela thought about how she contributed to her grandmother's need for caregiving, she remembered how her grandmother in earlier years had been a vibrant and outgoing person, very involved with her church, civic and social organizations. Tangela's grandmother loved to do crafts and dance. As her health declined, her grandmother became more limited in the activities she enjoyed. It was hard for Tangela to watch this change as she had always experienced her grandmother as a woman on the go.

The change over time was in Tangela's grandmother's behavior and worsening memory. Her grandmother was subsequently diagnosed with a type of dementia. Because Tangela lived so far away, she could not fulfill the role of primary caregiver. Her aunt, who was Tangela's grandmother's eldest child and only living daughter, lived an hour from her grandmother, took on that role.

Other intermittent caregivers included Tangela's uncle who lived within three blocks of her grandmother's apartment and several siblings and cousins who lived within the immediate area.

One aspect of Tangela's caregiving was to speak by phone to her grandmother several times a week in the early and middle stages of her dementia. As her grandmother lost the ability to communicate, Tangela still contacted her once a week.

In order to maintain as much contact as possible, Tangela tried to travel to the East Coast at least two times a year to visit. Before her grandmother was placed in an assisted living facility, Tangela contributed financially to the 24-hour in-home care or basic living expenses.

Tangela describes the care she provided was to be more of an emotional support person to her aunt and uncle. Because Tangela's mother, their sister, had passed away, Tangela took on the role of being her voice on caregiving decision making with them.

Tangela is a self-employed professional; therefore, she was able to arrange her work schedule to be available for the family as they needed her. This flexibility became a major resource to family members who were more or less onsite.

Both of Tangela's daughters were minors during the period she was a caregiver. This, in some ways limited her travel because she was such a distance away from her immediate family. Tangela feels her daughters may have had to live with a little more emotional stress of knowing that they were at a distance from a family member who could have used their assistance. There were a few occasions when Tangela flew across country to help, but mainly she was a point of contact who could be readily reached.

Tangela also learned about how living with dementia can be so painful for family members, as her grandmother moved further into dementia she actually started talking more about her childhood. Tangela was fascinated to hear her tell stories about her younger life of which she was never aware. These included stories about her great-grandparents whom Tangela did not know. These stories turned out to be family heritage gifts that Tangela would have never known about otherwise.

Tangela's grandmother passed away several years ago. Tangela has, however, had time to reflect on how she might, given an opportunity to do a reset of her caregiving experience, would have relocated to be near her grandmother. This would have helped her be much more present to assist with her grandmother's needs. This also would have given more time to spend with her grandmother while she was still able to communicate, especially to tell her life stories.

In thinking about what she learned as a result of her caregiving experience, Tangela said, "Sadly, I learned that not everyone sees or handles their responsibilities at the same level. I had expectations of how family members who lived closer would participate in my grandmother's care. That did not manifest, which led to feelings of resentment."

"Of all the lessons I've learned through my years of caregiving, the most important is to keep the love connection going. Just tell them you love them again and again and again. You will never say it too much, ever."
— Joan Lunden (happyhealthycaregiver.com)

Unexpected Learnings

This account includes at least two major lessons that can be learned from caregiving from afar. While there were family members who lived close by, some could not be depended on to be primary caregivers. This is not an uncommon occurrence. Rather than spending time and energy lamenting others' lack of involvement, if you are the caregiver from afar you would serve yourself well and your loved one best by doing what you can do. Just think of the loss the non-involved loved ones experience by not giving of themselves in a time of need.

The second lesson was even though dementia is such a debilitating disease, the fact that one of the gifts, if accepted, is that often one's experiences of a younger time can be recalled and told with great clarity. Some family members have used these storytelling times to record these accounts to share with others. A rich family history message for sure.

Some caregivers have learned the value of joining support groups of families who have members with dementia diagnoses such as Alzheimer's Disease. It can be helpful to learn they are not alone in their journey of caring for a family member who has such a debilitating diagnosis. Participating in such a group can increase knowledge about how the illness can change the emotional makeup of a formerly pleasant loved one. Some groups bring in subject matter experts to educate participants about the various stages of the disease as well as resources available to support them throughout the stages of illness. Resources include those available at governmental agencies such as the National Institute on Aging online. A few titles available include *Alzheimer's Caregiving Tips; Caring for a Person with Alzheimer's Disease: Your Easy-to-Use Guide from the National Institute on Aging; Home Safety for People with Alzheimer's Disease; Tips for Managing Agitation, Aggression and Sundowning; Alzheimer's Caregiving: Caring for Yourself; Helping Family and Friends Understand Alzheimer's Disease.* These and other NIA resources can be found at www.nia.nih.gov/health. Copies of these resources can be ordered, many for free at the NIA website, or by calling 1-800-222-2225 (toll free) or 1-800-222-4225 for TTY (toll free).

Other Tips for Caregiving Action

If you don't have active family members, you may want to make a list of all friends or associates the person you care for knows. It is ideal to have family members assist; however, this may not always be the case. Therefore, there is nothing amiss with pulling from the village that surrounds you or your loved one.

- For example, maybe a neighbor can help one hour a day to do dishes.
- A church member can provide an encouraging word once a month and make a call on a regular basis "just to check in."

Chapter 4 Summary

❑ Rather than spending time and energy lamenting others' lack of involvement, if you are the caregiver from afar, you would serve yourself and your loved one best by doing what you can do.

❑ Even though dementia is such a debilitating disease, one of its gifts, if accepted, is that often one's experiences from a younger time can be recalled and told with great clarity.

Notes

Notes

FRANCIS' LONG DISTANCE CAREGIVING

"Francis was proud to share a local community magazine article published decades ago about how the family functions as a cohesive unit, with notations about how each member contributes to the well-being of the family."

Francis' long-distance caregiving is a story of loving care made possible by recognizing the value of staying in contact with her mother and the rest of her family from across the miles. Francis lives in a state in the western United States, her mother remains in their family home in far northeast. She describes her mother as being in generally good health.

About her mother's need for caregiving, Francis says:

"My mother is pretty self-sufficient. She does get a little confused and forgetful at times. She has, at times, made poor decisions (example: She went out and got a loan to replace the roof on her home without consulting with anyone.) Another decision was that she started communicating with a man who did not appear to have her best interest in mind.

Also, she began mismanaging her money. She would miss paying bills and was unable to account for some of her funds. She lives alone in the four-bedroom home in which she raised me, my older brother and a younger sister. The house is becoming more than she can handle, and she refuses to consider downsizing. She is also losing weight and we are concerned that she might not be eating enough."

Francis was proud to share a local community magazine article published decades ago about how the family functions as a cohesive unit, with notations about how each member contributes to the well-being of the family. Her sister lives about five minutes from their mother. Her sister has also been very supportive and has taken the lead on checking in on their mother. Francis' brother lives about 15 minutes away and keeps close contact with their mother as well. He maintains contact with their mother once or twice a week. In addition, he ensures their mother's driveway and walkway are cleared of snow that occurs frequently in their city.

Francis, who fulfills the role of a secondary caregiver, estimates she devotes about 20 hours each month in caregiving for their mother. She does this daily by phone and by visiting their mother at least two times a year. Sometimes, more often if needed. This investment in time is the primary personal cost for this privilege of caring for the one who invested so much in Francis' and her siblings' well-being. Francis describes the nature of the care she provides to their mother as overseeing financial and medical matters. She estimates the financial investment for their mother as approximately $1,000 each year.

Francis states her caregiving experience has very little impact on her demanding employment as an upper-level manager. She feels fortunate to having an employer that is very supportive when she needs leave time to participate in caregiving matters with their mother.

Francis states her caregiving responsibility has had very little impact on family life. She describes her single, 24-year-old daughter as pretty self-sufficient.

The Village Proverb

This brief caregiving story is an example of how the "It Takes a Village" proverb, popularized in 1996 Hillary Clinton book about childrearing, can apply to adult caregiving. The exact origin of this phrase is unsubstantiated, however the proverb "It takes a village to raise a child," has its origins on the African continent. This proverb speaks to an entire community — all its people coming together, pooling resources, networking and interacting for the sake of the children. In order for children to grow up strong and healthy in a safe environment, the village looks out for all children.

The village proverb is relevant to adult caregiving when a family acts as a cohesive unit, with each taking responsibility to do a part of what it takes to ensure the well-being of a loved one in need of assistance. One strategy for the Village to take is to convene a meeting of family members, preferably including the person needing care, to discuss how each aspect of care will be carried out, when and to what extent. A record of the meeting results should be documented and passed out to each participant with a place on it for each person to sign an agreement with the content. Additionally, an agreement should be formalized as to how accountability for each aspect of care will be maintained on a defined basis.

Other Afar Action Options
- **Find a local coordinator**

  When caregiving from afar, it can be especially useful to have a local care manager who can supply local knowledge and help with caregiving logistics. One option is to hire a reputable professional — often called a geriatric care manager or eldercare navigator/coordinator. They can be especially valuable as objective mediators when family members disagree on care decisions and when you're facing tough choices, such as whether it's no longer safe for your loved one to live at home.

- **Find someone reliable.** Many people who identify themselves as care managers are unqualified for such a crucial role, so verify credentials. Consider years of experience and professional certifications. Resources include www.guardianship.org, www.csa.us and www.cmsa.org.
- **Discuss what they can do and their areas of expertise.** You can hire them for a few hours' consultation to develop a care plan or they can manage nearly the whole caboodle: from hiring and overseeing caregivers to taking on power of attorney for a loved one who is reluctant to designate a family member and may prefer a professional.
- **Consider cost.** Health insurance may not cover their services, and they typically charge anywhere from $50 to $200 an hour. But an experienced care manager may be able to save your family time, money and stress with even a brief consultation.

- **Stay in the loop.** Establish regular ways to communicate with your local team and loved one, whether through various organization apps, group emails or social tools like FaceTime, Skype, or Zoom. If doctors don't have the time or inclination to follow up with you after meeting with your loved one, you'll need to be both assertive and creative to stay plugged in.

Other Tips

- **Make good use of technology.** With your loved one's permission (or her legal proxy's), you can implement tools like video monitors and wearable activity trackers. Also available: remote door locks (to prevent wandering in case of dementia) and even electronic pill dispensers that can notify you if someone has taken their medications.
- **Stay clued in to doctors' orders.** The person you're caring for might not remember everything important discussed

during a doctor's appointment (who does?). You might suggest taking a digital recorder so that you can listen later, or to bring a friend to take notes.

- **Consider easy ways to coordinate.** Set up an email group you can use to keep everyone up to date. You might use an online scheduling tool such as Lotsa Helping Hands (https://lotsahelping-hands.com/) to organize and stay current on who's doing what and when.

- **Look into workplace leave policies.** You may be eligible for time off from work for caregiving under the Family and Medical Leave Act (if you work for a small company or haven't worked for your employer long, you may not be). As a compromise, some caregivers arrange to work remotely when they leave town for a caregiving visit.

Make the Most of Visits

Nothing replaces an in-person visit. So, when you can manage one, come with a list of things you need to know or discuss. Try to stretch the visit so you can spend time with your loved one, but also are able to schedule key face-to-face appointments related to their well-being. Sitting down to chat with someone is far more personal and revealing than a phone call can ever be.

- **Meet current and potential service providers.** You may want to interview potential home health aides or house-keepers or meet with social workers or other health care professionals involved in caregiving, to discuss any concerns.

- **Note where new help is needed.** Is a faucet dripping or the lawn overgrown? Does your loved one appear to be having trouble doing certain chores, such as laundry or grocery shopping? You can help with some tasks while you're there but may now need to find someone local to assist day-to-day.

- **Look for signs of abuse.** Ask your loved one if you can see his checking account and look for abnormalities. Other red flags: bruises and other unexplained injuries, or an abrupt change in personality. Be very concerned if he mentions someone you've never met who visits often and has been "helpful."

- **Have fun together.** While you might have many practical tasks to check off your list, it's important to spend quality time with your loved one, who may have decreased mobility and feel isolated. Set aside a few hours to go out to eat or to the movies, or maybe invite neighbors over for a potluck.

Chapter 5 Summary

- ☐ Recognize the value of staying in contact.

- ☐ Know that you are not alone.

- ☐ There is value in joining a support group, especially in the case of Alzheimer's.

Notes

Notes

ALEXANDRIA'S STORY

"My dad didn't share much. He was mean and grouchy. He would say things to hurt my feelings. I would have to remember he didn't mean what he was saying, but it was hard to hear hurtful words and name calling."

Alexandria was excited when she was awarded a new job at a location 1,700 miles away from the city she had grown up and worked in since she was a youngster. She had recently earned a bachelor's degree and was ready to "spread her wings" as a professional in the field of her choice. When Alexandria relocated, she realized that the caregiving she had given to her father, then in his late 70s, and her grandmother, in her 90s, who lived together, would be different. As long as she lived in her hometown Alexandria checked in on them daily and shared caregiving responsibilities on a regular basis. One of her eight brothers, Ron, had been his father's and grandmother's live-in caregiver for some time. One other relative, a niece, was also a part-time caregiver. While other siblings would drop by occasionally to see their father and grandmother, none took on responsibility of being caregivers. Ron would complain to Alexandria that none of the other brothers would help him with caregiving; their response was that if he needed help, he should ask for it.

Alexandria described her memories of her loved ones:

"My grandmother was quiet and didn't complain. She would tell me the same stories over and over of how she picked cotton and learned to quilt, which I loved to hear. After a while I recognized she was showing signs of dementia, which was a problem. In the year of her death her foot was broken, and my brother didn't notice it. On a visit to check on them I saw her foot was obviously swollen and inflamed. I asked our grandmother if it was painful. She replied, "No, it doesn't hurt." When we took her to a doctor it was too late to do anything about it because the infection had spread throughout her body. She died a short time later at age 104."

"My dad didn't share much. He was mean and grouchy. He would say things to hurt my feelings. I would have to remember he didn't mean what he was saying, but it was hard to hear hurtful words and name calling."

"His mother passed away two years before he did, when he was 82 years old. His last words to me were that he would never forgive me for giving away his sofa. The sofa was nasty, soiled with body fluids and other waste, so I disposed of it in the trash. I thought I was doing a good thing when I bought him a recliner to replace the sofa. What I didn't consider is that my grandmother sat on the sofa next to him. I thought I was doing something nice, but by throwing out the sofa I was erasing the memory he had of his mother. I didn't realize this until my father passed away about two years later. I would fight with my dad over the phone about silly things and wouldn't talk with him for a few days. Looking back, I didn't have to engage with or get so upset with him. I now know when someone is not feeling well, it may change their mental capacity."

Alexandria found the out-of-state responsibilities to be quite expensive and stressful, because she had to use all the employer-provided leave time to care for her grandmother and dad. She made a habit of flying to the family's home several times a year to give her brother Ron a break. She would take on any of the tasks that he was doing throughout the time she was in town. Alexandria said: "Living so far away made care-giving difficult. I was thankful my brother was living with them. Without him being present I would have had to move closer to them."

Alexandria shared lessons learned as a result of her caregiving experience:

- When you truly love someone, you can find the strength inside to do what it takes to make them comfortable and make sure they are okay.
- Be patient.
- Take a break to allow time for yourself.
- Have unconditional love.
- Ask for help.
- Prepare financially for caregiving.

Getting Help from Reluctant Others

Based on what occurred in Alexandria's family, in which one sibling out of eight was the sole consistent caregiver, there are a number of approaches other families have found beneficial.

- One is to call a family meeting to discuss caregiving needs and to cite what can be most helpful to the primary caregiver. Spelling out what is currently being done and what is needed to fill in the gaps can be enlightening.

- In some cases, asking one person to take on tasks such as ensuring that the loved one's bills are paid on time on a regular basis will lighten the load of the person who has been taking on that chore.

- If there is a need for someone to ensure the lawn is cut regularly, another person can do that themselves or hire someone else to do so.

- Arranging to have wholesome meals prepared or delivered a certain number of times each week can be of great benefit.

- In a large family like Alexandria's, a commitment by each person to check on the loved one with a brief visit or a regular phone call may be welcomed.

- An unexpected greeting card or small gift on a holiday or birthday of the loved one can brighten the day, and the attitude of the loved one and primary caregiver.

- Finally, asking reluctant others to suggest things they can do to help may result in a number of other suggestions, such as an offer to give the primary caregiver a day away from their responsibilities.

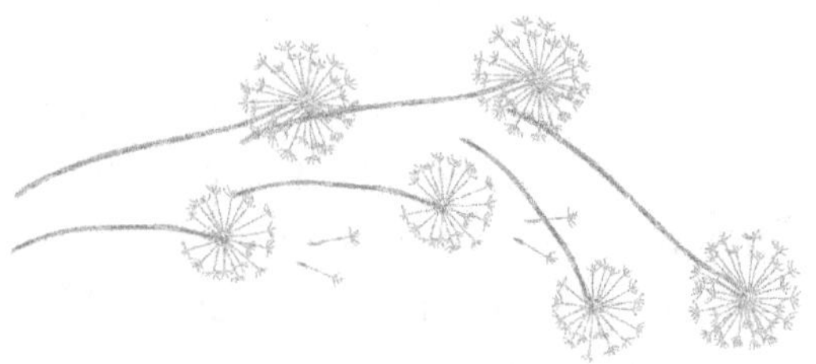

Chapter 6 Summary

- ❑ When you truly love someone, you can find the strength to do what it takes to make them comfortable and ensure they are okay.

- ❑ Be patient.

- ❑ Show unconditional love.

- ❑ Take a break allow time for yourself.

- ❑ Ask for help.

- ❑ Prepare financially for caregiving.

Notes

Notes

7.

NEVA'S CAREGIVING

*"Neva again tried to talk to her mother about
leaning less on neighbors and enlisting services
of a healthcare agency for short visits, at bedtime
and in the mornings."*

ach time Neva made caregiving trips to her mother's home, it was 260 miles, with difficult driving over mountain passes at times during severe weather conditions. While this was a trip to the town she grew up in, it was always a bit of a challenge.

How Neva Determined Her Mother Needed Caregiving Support

Neva's father passed away when her mother was around 81. Her mother had been Neva's dad's caretaker for the last few years of his life, and she was tired. His passing was also very hard for her mother emotionally since they had been married almost 60 years. Neva's mom always missed him, yet she regained energy and was very active in many community groups and an involved member of her church. Her mom kept busy and was connected to many friends. She was fairly independent throughout her 80s and even in her early 90s. During this period, Neva's mom had already contacted a service that provided very low-cost house cleaning for seniors, and she arranged for a lawn service.

Neva would take care of some things for her mom when she would visit for a few days, e.g., gardening, recycling and large trash pick-up, and helping her with bigger maintenance decisions. It was also during this time that Neva realized her mom was scooting up the stairs by sitting down because her knees were so bad. She spent time with her mother at two different times when she had knee replacement and started physical therapy. Her mom worked hard on her therapy with help of friends and had a great recovery.

During this period, Neva would visit her mom about every three months or so. As her mom grew older, Neva saw gradual changes in her mother's ability to get around, although she continued to be incredibly active. When her mother turned 95, Neva planned a big birthday party at the social hall at their First Methodist Church. Neva states her mother was very spry and happy at the party.

Over time Neva's trips were becoming more frequent. She tried to encourage her mother to get a little more help at home, but stated she was very stubborn and wouldn't have anything to do with it. Her mother was still driving (at age 95), and while Neva could see dents and scrapes on her car there were no accident reports of which she was aware. It was shortly afterwards that Neva learned her mother had been asking neighbors to come over to help her to go up the stairs to bed. Fortunately, Neva's cousins, friends and neighbors were all reliable and responsive. If Neva happened to call and couldn't reach anyone, she would request one of the other people in her network to stop by and check on her mom. A few of the caregivers gave Neva their phone numbers, so she could reach them as needed.

Neva learned there were a couple of times when her mother fell and pulled herself to the phone to call one of the people in their network for assistance. Also, she and her mom had connected with a service she could call. It did not involve wearing an emergency alert necklace, because her mother refused to wear one. After a while, Neva was concerned that her mother might be leaning too much on the next door neighbor, in particular. Her neighbor was raising kids and always seemed overwhelmed. At times, her mom would also call Neva's cousin and her husband to help in similar ways.

One night, her mom somehow rolled out of her bed and couldn't get back up. She was able to scoot to the nearby phone and call her cousin, and her husband came over to help. Although these incidents were infrequent, they were concerning.

Around this time, Neva again tried to talk to her mother about leaning less on neighbors and enlisting services of a healthcare agency for short visits, at bedtime and in the mornings. She was more open to this arrangement, relieving the neighbors and assuring that she felt safe at those times. Because her mother had a little savings, she and Neva discussed options of spending it on some caregiving services and other living needs and then applying for Medicaid caregiving once she could get certified to receive those services.

Around this time, a dear friend of Neva's had started stopping by every few days to check on Neva's mother. One morning, her friend found Neva's mom had slept on the couch in the living room. With covers still over her, Neva's mom told her friend that she just couldn't go up the stairs. When her friend called Neva, she was adamant that Neva make the 260-mile trip as soon as possible.

Shortly thereafter Neva started going with her mom on doctor visits. Her physician for several years had retired, and she was seeing a young, very caring doctor whom she liked very much. Neva found that she could contact him with questions and concerns as needed.

With the agency Neva retained, there were some nursing staff who would come by to assist Neva's mother who were very kind and helpful to her. Several of my mom's younger church members would also come by to assist as needed.

How Often Neva Made Contact with Her Mother

Before Neva and her mother engaged the caregiving agency, she made contact at least once a week. After they engaged the agency, Neva would call her mother every 2-3 days when helpers were scheduled to be there. As things progressed, Neva called every day or every other day, and particularly if she was aware that something was going on that might have been of concern. The best helpers would initiate contact with Neva if her mom wanted to talk to her or if they had concerns.

Neva's employment was ¾ time. She found that the best arrangement was for her to work three weeks and spend the fourth week at her mom's home. She would take personal unpaid time off from her job to go more frequently as needed.

The Nature of Care Neva Provided Versus That Provided by Others

Neva would take her mother to doctor's appointments and take care of other healthcare needs, such as picking up prescriptions, when she was in town. She also had direct communication with her mother's doctor. Neva would give her mother "shower baths," cut and wash, and put a permanent in her hair, when it was time to do so. Neva took her mother grocery shopping until she was not able to make those trips, then Neva generally did all of the shopping alone, stocking up for the times she would not be in town. Eventually, when Neva and her mother had helpers come in to prepare meals, Neva left notes for meal suggestions. Whenever Neva was there with her mother, she canceled or reduced the visits from the healthcare staff and tended to her mother's various needs and activities of daily living.

Anticipating that she would need/want to be available, Neva reduced her consulting work availability and took a part-time job. Although her job description was for part-time (salaried), she soon learned that her employer wanted at least full-time performance for the level of salary she received.

Caregiving Assistance Challenges

Once her mom went on Medicaid, Neva found she didn't have any say-so as to who could go by and check on her mom. Neva didn't find some of them helpful in the services they provided.

At one point, Neva was accused of elder abuse by the lead Medicaid staffer because she was unable to come to check on her mom more often than the staffer felt Neva should. This person and Neva ended up in a meeting called by this staffer in her mom's living room in which family friends at this meeting who had been coming to check on Neva's mom and provide assistance had to interrupt and dispute the comments being made by the Medicaid staffer. These friends were able to correct erroneous statements made by the employee, and to make statements of how Neva had made frequent contacts with them and others in the community to ensure her mother's caregiving needs were being addressed.

There were several things Neva learned about herself as a result of her caregiving experience. One of the primary lessons was that it was okay to ask for and receive help. The experience reinforced that she loved her mother unconditionally in spite of earlier issues. Quite frankly, Neva was grateful having done some personal self-care work on those issues when she was younger.

Neva assured her mother she would do everything she could to make it possible for her to stay at home. She also talked to her mother about coming to live with her as one option if it would be needed. She also applied for a couple of jobs in her hometown and explored whether she could get sufficient consulting work there.

Chapter 7 Summary

❑   Support is done in many ways.

Notes

SARAH'S FIRST-PERSON CAREGIVING ACCOUNT

"…in how everyone has their own creative and loving ways of giving and caregiving. We have to learn how to be flexible in how caregiving is delivered."

During the last ten years, Dad had been receiving support from my sister. As his short-term memory began to fail, the one-to-one care increased. Medications had to be more closely monitored, simple errands, and a variety of doctor visits were needed.

As for me, it is difficult not being able to help an aging parent who resides in another state. Of course, as we know, there is also concern regarding the welfare of the caregiver. My sister devoted much of her "spare time" to fulfilling Dad's every need. I tried a variety of ways to support the caregiver process of my father... and... my sister. For instance, I sent restaurant and movie gift cards as a simple thank you to my sister for all the care she was giving. These gift cards also assisted with outings for Dad. I also increased the number of phone calls to give Dad more attention. He particularly enjoyed talking with the grandchildren and my husband. Those voices and light conversation made life more enjoyable and was good for his overall health and mind and morale. Special thank you notes and drawings from the grandchildren to both Dad and my sister always brought smiles and laughter; especially, when the situation seemed to be difficult. Of course, as time and finances permitted, I increased the visitations to California to check on both of these very important people.

I learned that I am probably going to feel some level of guilt, from time-to-time, but I know that I cannot be all things to every one of my family members and friends. Prioritizing needs and support is a challenge in our daily lives. When you cannot be nearby to care take 24/7, it forces you to become creative in your support. I learned that I had to accept and trust that my sister was making the best decisions possible, at the time. I learned that I am a good listener. Sometimes just listening is the best way to assist and support. Allowing someone to be able to share and vent without judgment is also a way of being supportive near or far.

When my dad passed away, he had lived a full life and I knew that he was loved and appreciated right up to the end. He was a good dad, and we were blessed to have had him for over 94 years. My sister and I are six years apart and have become more closely connected because of having to work together. We definitely know a lot more about each other. Not only have I learned some things about myself through this caregiving experience but I have a deeper understanding about my amazing sibling.

In summary, everyone has their own creative and loving ways of giving and caregiving. We have to learn how to be flexible in how caregiving is delivered.

Family Appreciation for Best Efforts

This beautiful caregiving account demonstrates how distance does not prevent thoughtful caregiving from afar. This first-person account shows how what might be considered simple actions contributed to the well-being of the author's father and her sister who was his primary caregiver. Ongoing communication and symbolic actions such as sending gift cards to be used by the two of them were appreciated and brought joy. Telephone calls, while not costly, made a difference in how her father and sister maintained loving connections.

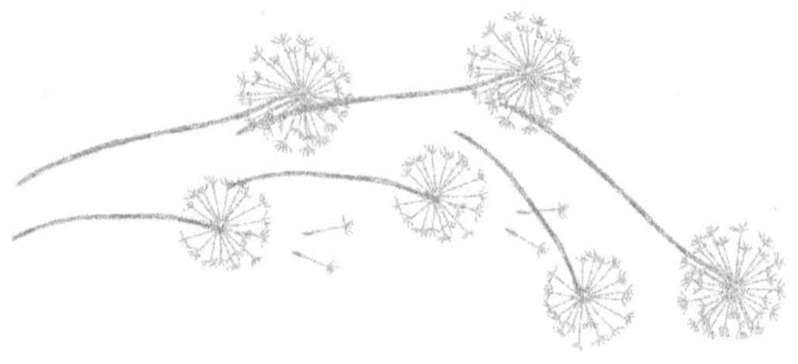

Chapter 8 Summary

☐ Distance does not prevent thoughtful caregiving from afar.

☐ Send gift cards to be used by both the caregiver and the receiver of care.

☐ Never underestimate the power of a phone call.

Notes

Notes

MAE'S CAREGIVING EXPERIENCE

"Important in this caregiving experience was Mae's commitment to maintain the quality of her own health. Whenever she would visit her aunt, she always took advantage of her health club membership to exercise regularly."

Aunt Gigi was Mae's dad's youngest sister and for many years the primary caregiver for her mother, father, and older sister. Basically, over the years her aunt took care of everyone in her family. In her late 70s her health began to fail. At some point, Aunt Gigi expressed concern that no one was left to take care of her in time of need. Her aunt did not have children of her own, so she often referred to Mae as her daughter. Mae lived several states away but promised Aunt Gigi she would never be alone and she would always take care of her, no matter the circumstances. Over the years, this required Mae to make frequent phone calls and flights from the western state in which she resides to her aunt's home in Texas every other month, and sometimes more often.

Aunt Gigi had multiple chronic health problems, resulting in episodes that sent her to the hospital several times each year. Each time, Mae went to Texas to be with her during the hospital stay. Mae found it ironic that with many nieces and nephews in her hometown or nearby, Aunt Gigi would call her when hospitalized. Of note, is that Mae's skill as a nurse practitioner enhanced her ability to serve as her aunt's long-distance caregiver, even though she lived more than 1,000 miles away. With their knowledge of Mae's professional background, armed with a healthcare power of attorney (POA), doctors at all of the healthcare facilities were generous in making phone calls to her and responsive to her calls and emails. With the POA legal designation, Mae was also tasked with making medical decisions if Aunt Gigi became incapacitated in any way or unable to communicate her own healthcare decisions. This allowed Aunt Gigi's physicians to share information about her medical status electronically as needed. Mae learned that creating a paper trail of all of these contacts helped her be effective as a long distance caregiver.

During Aunt Gigi's' early stages of her chronic heart disease, she also developed chronic kidney failure. This required additional hospitalizations and changes in her diet and medications. Mae taught her the specifics of prescribed dietary restrictions and would watch her prepare meals to ensure she was complying with them. Mae found that these multiple ailments took a toll on her personality as at times she became somewhat demanding and disagreeable. Sometimes the caregiving tasks became quite difficult. For instance, Aunt Gigi she would say hurtful things and apologize later. Mae finally realized she needed to tell her when she felt hurt at the time this occurred.

Mae made a point of visiting Aunt Gigi for a few days before major holidays like Thanksgiving and Christmas, holidays their family always shared together with great food and fellowship. Because Mae loves to cook, she always visited her just before these holidays and made her favorite meals. Aunt Gigi always commented about how great this was and how much she appreciated these special caregiving gifts.

Due to her heart condition and chronic kidney failure, Aunt Gigi qualified for remote blood pressure checks via telemeter and heart checks via Tele-electrocardiogram. All of this was set up in her home in a little town of 4,000 people. All Aunt Gigi had to do was dial the clinic number and put her blood pressure cuff on and let it do its thing. She thought this was really cool.

In addition to caring for Aunt Gigi's healthcare needs, Mae also became her aunt's financial power of attorney and manager. Mae got access to the information she needed to pay Aunt Gigi's bills online and eventually paid all of them electronically from her home desk. Mae made quarterly reports of Aunt Gigi's financial status and medical and physical status to agencies such as Medicare and Medicaid, which funded her aunt's healthcare services. Mae would fly to Aunt Gigi's home several times per month or at each change in her health status to ensure all her needs were addressed.

Aunt Gigi would call Mae almost every day or Mae would call her every other day just to check on and reassure her. Mae found her aunt to be compulsively organized, which facilitated establishing a routine for her medications, her special dietary needs and her regular visits to her doctors. Mae taught Aunt Gigi the specifics for all her medication, which Aunt Gigi memorized over time and would repeat the purpose of each to Mae.

Important in this caregiving experience was Mae's commitment to maintain the quality of her own health. Whenever she would visit her aunt, Mae always took advantage of her health club membership to exercise regularly. She also continued her daily early morning walks that were part of her daily routine when she was at home. Mae found this helped her deal with the stress she felt in taking care of someone with a chronic condition while in Aunt Gigi's hometown and from afar. She relates that taking care of her Aunt taught her the importance of patience, perseverance, and empathy.

<u>Special Note: The POWER of Powers of Attorney</u>
A key to Mae's success as long distance caregiver was the supplement of having both financial and healthcare powers of attorney. The financial power of attorney (POA) allowed Mae to take financial actions on Aunt Gigi's behalf

under circumstances defined in the POA. This document gave her legal authority to act as her aunt's attorney-of-fact or agent. Having this authority allowed her to make the decisions that she felt were in keeping with her aunt's wishes and financial well-being. Having this authority took the burden of these potentially stressful decisions off her ailing aunt.

The healthcare power of attorney (HCPA) also gave Mae the legal authority to make health-related decisions and to get feedback and input from doctors and others who were involved in Aunt Gigi's care. This document named Mae as the one person to serve as her aunt's healthcare agent or proxy. As the designated proxy, Mae was entrusted with the power and responsibility to make decisions about her aunt's medical care under circumstances outlined in the document. The exact decision-making responsibilities were spelled out in detail. Because of Aunt Gigi's confidence in Mae's healthcare knowledge and her belief that any decisions or actions she would take on her behalf would be the right ones, she leaned heavily on Mae throughout her many years of serious illness.

Related Background Information

Naming a healthcare proxy is an extremely important decision. Living nearby is not a requirement to be a healthcare proxy. Even a long-distance caregiver can be one. Most people ask a close friend or family member to be their healthcare proxy. Some people turn to a trusted member of the clergy or a lawyer. The person chosen should be able to understand the treatment choices, know loved one's values, and support their decisions.

Another document that needs to be executed is the advance directive, which spells out actions to be taken if the person needing care is not able to speak for themselves. It is wise to let the family member or other loved ones know that this is a document that can be revised and/or updated as often as they wish. Patients and caregivers should discuss these decisions—and any changes in them—and keep the healthcare team informed. Copies of advance directives should be given to all caregivers and a copy should be kept at home as well. Because state laws vary, it is wise to check with the local Area Agency on Aging, state department of aging, or a lawyer for more information about advance directives.

The *Five Wishes* is an example of documenting advance directive about health care. The document is available at https://www.fivewishes.org/for-myself/.

Chapter 9 Summary

- ❑ Know the importance of:

  P - Patience

  P - Perseverance

  E - Empathy

- ❑ Continue your exercise regimen, especially your early morning walks.

- ❑ Consider a healthcare proxy; living nearby is not a requirement.

- ❑ Consider obtaining the power of attorney:

  - ▫ Financial power of attorney

  - ▫ Healthcare power of attorney

Notes

Notes

ANDRE'S CAREGIVING STORY

"He made the journey to her home almost every weekend; sometimes during week days, depending on her health condition."

When Andre was growing up in his small southeastern United States town, he knew his mother was widely respected in their community. She was revered as a "community mother", "church mother", and activist who made changes in early childhood education and well-being of young children. It was not until he was in his middle age years that he became aware of how the nurturing attention she gave to him and his five siblings would provide the basis for him knowing how to take care of her needs in her later years.

His mother, Mrs. W, who was born in 1914, seemed to have always known how to make a difference in the lives of others in her close knit town. She took loving care of her children as well as her husband, who passed away in 1985. It was during the years of his father's illness, that Andre became aware of the intricacies of caregiving. At that time he was completing a military assignment at a base located about an hour and a half from his hometown. Recognizing his mother's need for help with his father's activities of daily living, Andre would leave his assignment on weekends to help his mother. At that time, his mother, still in her early middle age years was very appreciative of what was a sacrifice by a young man to help with tasks she could not do on her own.

Mrs. W was so revered in her town that her pastor remarked that the church belonged to her. After her passing at age 100, Andre became more aware of how much she meant, not only to the local community, but her state as a whole. Several years earlier, she had been selected by researchers at a major university in their state to have her life history digitally archived as a living legend icon, to be remembered throughout the state. Andre feels honored that he can still actually hear his mother's voice, telling her own story for years to come.

In the early 2000s, Andre decided to relocate to his home state, in part to be closer to his mother. Several years before, glaucoma had robbed her of much of her eyesight, making her more dependent on others to take care of daily activities. Andre's new residence was about 200 miles away from her mother's home. While it was quite a distance from his mother's home, Andre was much closer than the more than a thousand miles of his former residence for more than a decade. This new proximity made it easier for him to reach her within a few hours, rather than a day or more from that earlier location. The job he held in his new location also let Andre have the freedom to make decisions as needed to go to his mother's side.

While one of Andre's siblings provided some assistance with caregiving responsibilities, others did so on a more or less hit or miss basis. This was frustrating for him but did not deter him from being at this mother's side whenever she needed him. Andre was particularly grateful for the part-time home care services provided by governmental agencies to assist with activities of daily living. His state of mind was also eased knowing that his mother's circle of friends was available to assist with her caregiving needs when necessary.

Andre traveled on weekends to check on his mother and take her to doctor appointments. A series of factors made him determine he needed to step up long distance caregiving on his part. His brother's work schedule would not allow him to do these things. In addition, Andre recognized that he had an easier time recognizing how to provide emotional as well as his mother's physical needs. He made the journey to her home almost every weekend; sometimes during week days, depending on her health condition.

Andre's mother lived in an historical black community in which personal relationships were traditionally very close. Because of this, there was a dependable network of family friends who were available to provide a continuum of care until he could get there. Mrs. W was well known across her religious denomination. She knew generations of children. He states she earned an unusual level of respect, because of being well known for her devotion to her community.

In reflecting on what he learned from his caregiving experience, Andre expressed a number of thoughts. One is that love is about more than words. He states you have to show it. It may not be convenient but he learned from his mother how to express love; how to consider the interests of others: "Never let anybody thank you for doing the right thing. I pray, thanking God for letting me be her son."

Andre stated that if he had the opportunity to start the caregiving experience again, he would let very little get in his way. He feels he would be more self-sacrificing. His mother would always be his first priority. He remembers fondly her saying, "You're the only one of my children who gives me roses."

Chapter 10 Summary

- ❑ The best way forward will evolve as you go along.

- ❑ Navigation is more important than speed.

- ❑ A team approach is the key to success.

- ❑ Conditions change along the way, and your strategies will shift accordingly.

- ❑ Get the support you need.

- ❑ Respect your loved one's expressed values and preferences.

- ❑ Stay in good condition yourself; caregiving is a long-term

commitment, so take care of
yourself.

❑   As much as possible, involve the
person who needs care in the
decision-making process.

Notes

Notes

FROM CAREGIVING SURVEYS TO CAREGIVING STORIES

Other than for my caregiving account about Aunt Clea, each person who contributed a caregiving story was sent a survey to complete about their experiences as *Caregivers From Afar*. In some cases, the survey was completed as a telephone interview. Other times it was completed as an interview conversation, which was recorded as we spoke. The survey account below was completed totally in written form. Most survey results are summarized. Rather than summarizing this one, to preserve its richness, the complete survey is presented with the care-giver's permission. Their identity, as well as that of her family members, is kept anonymous. Also, anything in this kind of space _____ is a minor editorial update to maintain anonymity.

L.A.'s Completed Survey

1. **What was your relationship to the person to whom you provided long-distance caregiving?**
    - She was, and always will be, my mother, Mrs. D.E.

2. **What was the approximate distance you lived from person you provided care?**
    - 2700 miles or about a 40 hour drive.

3. **What made you determine that he or she needed caregiving?**
    - My mom used to come up north and spend 4, 6 or 8 weeks with me, my son and husband yearly at around

the same time of the year. With
each of these years and even when I
would go home for various events, I
was witnessing her increasing frailty.
One year when she was at our home
and I was at work, she called me to
say that she accidently flooded our
kitchen floor. I truly wondered how
that could have happened, but I
came home quickly and indeed, the
linoleum-covered floor had A LOT of
water on it. She was very apologetic.
I mopped it all up and asked her
questions to find out how this could
have happened. Finally, I determined
that she'd been in the kitchen washing
dishes, had gotten tired of standing so
she decided to go into the living room
to sit on the couch and rest a bit. It
seems she left the water running in
the kitchen sink and left the drain
closed so when the water reached the
top it started spilling onto the floor.
Eventually she woke up and returned

to the kitchen to find the floor covered in water. She proceeded to walk through the water-- I'm sure she did not have her walker with her-- to turn off the faucet. She then called me. We laughed about it later and I told her that the kitchen floor had NEVER been that clean before and would probably never be again. I note that she did NOT share this story with my siblings when she spoke with them over the following weeks. While this was going on I also reflected on how many times in my life my precious mother had been there to make my mishaps…not so final. This experience, however, was insight into my mother's frailness and increased need to not be alone.

4. **What help did you have providing care?**
   - I am one of 7 children…now one of 6 children because our oldest

brother died while my parents were of sound mind and still healthy. I am the youngest and I live the farthest away from 'home'. The oldest sibling, several years before my parent's health was declining and based on a conversation among the siblings, agreed to move from __ to __, in anticipation of a time when our parents would need greater care and attention. The other siblings, to varying degrees, made it a practice to make sure we were coming home on a regular basis to be with our parents, and then to rotate going home, if some major health event/hospitalization/etc., occurred and required longer term support. We did this, and I emphasize to varying degrees depending on who the sibling was, so that the sibling who lived at home would not get totally burnt out/ feel put upon/get mad at the rest of us for not picking up some of the responsibility.

- I want to acknowledge that I was not her primary caregiver. My oldest sister who had moved home to be there for our parents was the primary caregiver. I want to also acknowledge that my second oldest brother, who lived in _____, was my parent's rock of Gibraltar. In every way you could need or imagine, he took his role as caregiver for my parents as they aged, seriously and he was in _____ every 4-8 weeks to take them to doctor's appointments, manage the house so my sister would not be overwhelmed, deal with their taxes and other business issues, take care of her vehicle, take her out to wherever she wanted to go when he was there, take my mom out to dinner when she complained about the food at the independent living facility where she

was living and a host of other caregiving things that would crop up.

○ I also want to let the world know
about my amazing sister-in-law.
Married to the brother I just
mentioned above. A better
daughter-in-law to my mother
could not have been found. She
and my brother were this united
team in caring for my father, while
he was alive and simultaneously,
for my mother up to her death. My
sister-in-law, in my opinion, was a
way better caregiver than I was. She
and my mom talked regularly. If there
was any and I mean any need that
my mom had, this daughter-in-law
was on top of it for my mom. She
knew the names of all my mom's
physicians and their physician assis-
tants. She knew the name of every
nurse or healthcare professional that
had anything to do with my parents.
She knew all my mom's (parents)

medications and during the time either parent traveled she made sure all their meds were ready, organized, listed along with their doses and times to be taken. She arranged wheelchair service going and coming from the airport. If my mom had a need this daughter-in-law had no limits to making sure her need was met.

5. **About how often did you have contact with your loved one who received care?**

   - I wish I could say weekly. When I was at home or when mom was up north with us, it was daily. When neither of these events was in play, I called home. I wish I could tell you I called home weekly but sadly, I did not. This is one of my regrets. I let my busy life get in the way of constantly staying in contact with my mom. If there was an issue to be addressed, I was focused and present but if not, I was in my corner of the world and would talk with my mom, periodically.

6. **What was the financial cost, if any, was there on you personally as a result of the need to provide caregiving for your loved one?**
   - The costs were almost exclusively connected to the travel to fly home, hotel stays if I did not stay at the family home, vehicle rentals if / when I did not drive her vehicle while I was home and food to eat if I was not eating with my sister or my brother during times when we were all there.
   - My mom, thankfully, had good health insurance.
   - There were a few times when we'd chip in for some purchase but not significant enough for me to put dollar figures to it.
   - What I know happened behind the scenes is, if there were costs

associated with increasing level of nursing support during her last months alive or even at points earlier during her healthcare, my brother and sister-in-law would be picking up the bill and not saying anything to us. I think because he knew what everyone else's financial situation was and decided that he would make it a non-issue.

7. **What was the nature of the care you provided versus that provided by others?**

   ◦ More than anything I feel my care was emotional support. For several years while she was still able she had a wonderful vacation spot to come to for 6-8 weeks out of the year. She looked forward to this getaway and so did we. She talked about it for months before she arrived and after she returned home. She hated the independent living facility where she lived and she said this let her look at four different walls. She met a whole new set of people at church and she bonded wonderfully with them and them with her. She attended ladies retreats with me, met the people I worked with and was simply able to slide into 'being back in a family home atmosphere. She needed that. Often when she came, I noted that she would get mad or frustrated about varying things and it would take her about a week of being here to be able to release some of those emotions.

- At this stage in MY life, we were able to talk about deep and insightful things and she was able to get some things off her chest, so to speak, that I know she'd had on her mind sitting in the independent living facility for a long time.

- When I was around my mom, we made sure to go get nails done and pedicures or massages. Sometimes I massaged her myself. I made sure to take her where she wanted to go and not rush her. When she came to our home up north, I made sure there were nights when I got in the bed with her and laid right next to her and put my arms around her while we slept because I knew those were experiences that would not be talked about but would also have not been happening in a long, long time.

- I understood my mom's spiritual foundation because mine came from her and so I wanted to make sure that spiritual events that she could go to…. we went to.

- I don't know if you'd call this care-giving or not, but there was a point when mom had knee surgery and the knee never did recover the way it needed to. This means she had not driven in a few years. One of her desires was to be able to drive her SUV again. Whenever I was with my mom I heard of this dream / desire over and over again. I also had heard my brother say that mom would not be driving again because she was not in a condition to be driving. One day I was taking my mom to the cleaners to pick up some items and this particular place was in a strip mall with a huge parking lot. Hearing my mom talk about how she longed to drive again and seeing this huge vacant parking lot, I said, "Mom, this looks like a good place for you to get behind the wheel and do a little driving." We switched seats, she got adjusted. I checked to make sure she still remembered what each part of the vehicle did and off she went driving around the parking lot. This little excursion quickly led to her driving out of the parking lot, around a few corners and we found ourselves right next to the freeway. Needless to say, I was terrified. All I could think

about was how I was going to explain
this to my siblings if anything tragic
happened. I calmly asked my mom
to get us back to the large parking
lot. We made it and I secretly decided
I'd never do that again. I don't know
if I ever told my siblings that story.
After that, however, my mother was
beaming with joy.

8. **What effect, if any, did your caregiving responsibilities have on
your work life?**

   - Because this was truly long distance.
   The impact went like this…. If I was
   planning to fly home, it would be on
   the heels of 50-60 hour/week work
   schedules. I'd be tired from work,
   only to fly home to relieve my sister,
   only to fly back home and pick up
   with a busy work schedule. Going
   home was never equated with rest.
   - What I did feel was guilt. I needed
   to be more present for mom, even

if it was simply to call and talk with her more regularly but my job was/is very demanding, and I let my job win and I did not stay in contact with my mom as much as I should have.

9. **What effect did caregiving have on your family and/or your life?**

   ◦ I am very thankful that my husband has always and even in the aging years welcomed my mom with open arms. Because he was supportive, when she came to visit with us annually, she would be at the house with him and would go around with him at times during the days she was here. My husband was the one who made sure we took annual trips home during the holidays to be with my parents.

   ◦ During times when my mom was able to spend time with us up north, this allowed her and our only son, to form a strong connection. He clearly knows his grandmother (on my side of the family) because these deliberate times even in caregiving occurred. When we were home for the holidays these times became caregiving times as well. My sister, who would have been the primary person, would be ready with, "I'm turning it over to you now." The effect of caregiving is that it allowed us to become closer to my mother. There were things she did need at this stage in her life, and we could provide it…. and I don't mean financial things… but relationship things. It helped my son gain experience in being present with the elderly and seeing life from the eyes of a person who has lived way longer than you have. My son now has stories of times he and his grandmother talked while being in our kitchen. This never would have occurred without her being up here. When we'd go home for the holidays, he was more comfortable to be with her and their relationship would just pick up and flow naturally. He knew how to help manage her walker or her belongings or just be patient around her…because he'd been some part of her caregiving when she was up north with us.

10. **Did you have minor children or others who were dependent on you?**
   ◦ Yes, our son, during mom's declining years would have been in middle to high school as time moved on.
   ◦ Because we lived so far away, the needs of our son did not create frustrations or challenges in caregiving.

11. **What happened if an emergency situation arose related to caregiving with your loved one?**
    - I'd fly home.
    - I'd put the flight on a credit card when funds were tight. Flying home to Vegas is not cheap on short notice.
    - My husband would pick up the slack at home while I was away.

12. **What did you learn about yourself or others as a result of your caregiving experience?**
    - I was blessed to have a mother like my mom.
    - People at church would see our interaction, during the times she was up here and it caused them to reflect on their – sometimes – not as positive relationships with their mom.
    - I needed to be more present for my mom. I was still quite selfish.

- ○ I can rise to the occasion and do what needs to be done with the right attitude.

13. **Can you think of one story about caregiving you remember most? Or other stories that may be of interest to others who find themselves in a caregiving situation?**

   - ○ For my mom's 91st birthday the siblings thought about what we would give my mom. We concluded that she needed NOT ONE THING, so we'd write her a book with our stories about her. We asked friends and people connected to her to share short stories if they wished. I had the pleasure of putting the book together and it was titled, ***"Chicken Soup for D.E.'s Soul" the 91st Birthday Edition,*** because she loved the Chicken Soup books and sent them to me regularly. The bound book was to arrive on her birthday (because of the mail a few days after) and it was THE BEST thing we ever could have given her. She read the book from cover to cover, several times, talked about it with ALL of us and disputed many of the stories in there. She said we did not have the facts right in some of those stories. She asked us to send it to her siblings. This book drew our family together in laughter and was our greatest collaborative project. When the siblings read the book, it allowed us to see things the other siblings valued or remembered that were not our memories. It was beautiful. In caregiving, take time to ask the parent to "tell me the time when….."

○ Also, my oldest sister was there when my mother took her last breaths and transitioned into eternal life. I so wished I'd been able to be there. My sister said, in some of those last days, "Mom said I see-- 'our older brother'-. My sister said, "where do you see him, mom?" Mom said, "Over there, standing right next to the bathroom door." I said, what else did you ask her? She did not ask her anything else. If your loved one is still in a state of being able to communicate those are the days indicating they are getting close to the end, don't be afraid to ask them what they see and what they are experiencing. My mother was a woman of faith and I wish I'd been there to keep asking her what she was experiencing and what she was seeing. People of Faith in God live their whole lives in view of this moment---ask them questions as they are walking this last mile of the way.

14. **What else would you like to share about the responsibility and opportunity to provide care to your loved one?**

   ◦ I am so glad God allowed me to be born to these two parents – ______ and _____. I am glad that I was able to be present for the times when I was present… I received more than I gave. I did not know that my mother was 'growing and maturing' me even as her health was declining but that is exactly what she was doing. So many of our shared experiences during her declining years was her getting me ready for a time when she would no longer be here on earth. Even now tears are coming to me. I am feeling selfish as I write this because I think this is supposed to be about my mom and I am writing this about me. My mom gave me such a great gift in her declining years and that gift was to help me get ready for life without her here on earth.... she did that subtly while she was living, through words of encouragement and insight and through little conversations that seemed unimportant. Now that she is gone, I know exactly how important those conversations were and I now see exactly what she was doing--- What an amazing and wonderful mother. This is what I plan to do in the life of my son. God help me!!!

15. **If you had the opportunity to start the caregiving experience again, what if anything would you have done differently?**

   ○ Call my mother. Take time for my mother. Don't think she will live forever. Stop working AS MUCH because the work will be there. Stop the other things that weren't that important and call my mother and talk to her and let her know, because I called, that I LOVE YOU. Return her phone calls more speedily. Not everyone gets a good mother. Don't take her for granted.

- I would have gotten in the bed with her more often and just hugged her until we both fell asleep. Older people get so few regular hugs and kisses. If the spouse has been sick and or has died there are those hugs and kisses that aren't there. We give older people quick hugs and kisses but we need to give them long, extended hugs. I call it the ONE MINUTE HUG. I hug you and in my head I'm counting the 60 seconds while gently rubbing your back and not saying anything… just giving you a warm embrace… for 60 seconds…and when you pull away you will hear me say, 39, 40, 41, 42, 43…we are not at 60 yet!!!!! I would have jumped in her bed and hugged her more often and longer and I would have given her more 60 second hugs.

16. **Other observations**
    - Thank you for this outlet to remember, in words, my beautiful precious mother.

Key Takeaways

- ❑ Rise to the occasion. Do what needs to be done with the right attitude.

- ❑ Call more often.

- ❑ Ask more questions as they walk the last few miles.

- ❑ Be more present.

- ❑ Take longer hugs.

Notes

Notes

FINAL THOUGHTS
ON CAREGIVING
ACTION PLANNING

There's no one right way to be a caregiver; there are many possibilities.

- The best way for you will evolve as you go along.
- Think of it as a journey: You'll take it step by step.
- Navigation is generally more important than speed— spending time at the beginning to understand your situation and your options will serve you better than rushing into action without a plan.

- Finding your way is a bit of a treasure hunt and a mental puzzle. A team approach is key to success.
- Conditions change along the way and your strategies will shift accordingly.
- Most of all, you will need to stay in good condition yourself for the long run.
  - If there are any rules to keep in mind: Take care of yourself.
  - This rule is the most important—yet family caregivers so often forget it.
  - Take a look at *Family Caregiver Alliance's Fact Sheet Taking Care of YOU: Self-Care for Family Caregivers.*
  - This publication offers suggestions about managing stress, setting goals, seeking solutions, communicating constructively and asking for and accepting help. (Note: all Family Caregiver Alliance publications are available at www.caregiver.org. See the References section at the end of this guide for more information.)

Knowledge and confidence will come a little at a time.

- Sometimes you have to take a step sideways, or even step backward, before you make progress. But bit by bit, you will sort out the challenges and find the solutions.
- Get the support you need. Support comes in many forms and from lots of places. What you find supportive is individual to you—the main thing is to not expect to "go it alone."
- As much as possible, involve the one who needs care in the decision-making process.
- Respect his or her expressed values and preferences, even when these differ from yours. Preventive Steps
- It will help you immeasurably if, before there is a crisis, your parent provides you with information to locate his or her records, important telephone contacts and other essential items.
- Where to Find My Important Papers is a one-page document available on the

FCA website (https://www.agis.com). It will help you collect information that will simplify communication with government agencies such as Social Security or the Veterans Administration; help with banking and other financial transactions; and make speaking with your parent's attorney or physician easier.

- Legal documents, such as Durable Powers of Attorney and Advance Directives, can and should be prepared before a medical condition makes it impossible to do so. See the FCA Fact Sheet Legal Issues in Planning for Incapacity for more information, or contact an elder law attorney.

- Sometimes, as you travel this road, you might think you need the skills and knowledge of a lawyer, accountant, doctor and social worker to make sense of things.

- Don't get discouraged! No one can master everything, not even the people who work full-time in the field.

- The solution lies in putting together a team and using each team member's strengths—including yours; getting the Lay of the Land, the sudden realization of your role as caregiver.

Diagnosis

Doctor List

Medication List

Diet

Clothing/Shoe Size

Notes

Notes

Notes

Notes

CAREGIVING FROM AFAR RESOURCE LIST

CHECKLIST/HANDBOOKS

- Handbook for Long-Distance Caregivers. www.Caregiver.org>Long_Distance _handbook
- Long Distance Family Caregiving: A Checklist – Human Good (https://www.humangood.org/ resources/senior-care-guides/ checklist-long-distance-caregiving
- Long Distance Caregiving/National Institute on Aging. www.nia.nih. gov>health>caregiving
- Eight Tips for Long-Distance Caregiving- National Institute on Health. www.nia. nih.gov>sites-default or www.nia.nih.gov/ longdistance-caregiving

- AARP Caregiving Resource Link. (1.877.333.5885 in English; 1.888.971.2013 in Spanish)

AGING/ALZHEIMERS/DEMENTIA

- Seven Stages of Alzheimer's. http://m.alz.org/stages-of-alzheimers.asp
- How to Help a Loved One with Alzheimer's When You Don't live Nearby. http://www.healthafter50.com/alerts/memory/Helping_Loved-One-Alzheimers-Not-Nearby
- National Institute on Aging Information Center. (Free information in English and Spanish) 1-800-222-2225 (toll free) niaic@nia.nih.gov (email) www.nia.nih.gov (website)

FAMILY CARE/RELATIONSHIPS

- How to Care for Your Aging Parent from a Distance. Money.usnews.com
- Top 3 Excuses From Siblings Who Don't Help With Caregiving by Carol Bradley, et.al. AgingCare.com

- 6 Ways to Make Sure Your Loved One's Home is More Secure by Amy Osmond Cook. https://www.agingcare.com/articles/6-ways-to-make-your-loved-ones-home-more-secure-211859.htm
- Conversation Starters: 20 Questions to Ask Your Parents by Marlo Sollitto. AgingCare.com .
- https://www.agingcare.com/Articles/ques-tions -to-ask -elderly-parents
- 4 Red Flags to Look for During Holiday Visits with Parents. https://www.aging-care.com/Articles/holiday-visits
- Caregiving from Afar: How Home Health Aides Can Be Your Lookout. Home Care now
- Aging Life Care Association. 1-520.881.8008. info@aginglifecare.org (email) www.againglifecare.org (website)

ABOUT THE AUTHOR

Mary McGlothin Davis, PhD, RN, has, for a long time been dedicated to caregiving of the elderly. Starting with serving as a staff development leader as registered nurse at a long-term facility in Northern Wisconsin to owning a 10-year licensed long-term agency in Colorado, she remains committed to advocating the best care possible for seniors. Serving as a professional nursing instructor at two colleges helped her hone her skill in making the most of time spent interacting with various audiences and cultures. Over the years, she has been called upon to speak to numerous groups about topics related to eldercare. In addition, she has published a variety of articles on topics of interest to caregivers.

Over the past 20 years, she became aware of how often family members do not live in close proximity with each other. This has often had a particular impact with younger relatives who live quite a distance from elders. The challenges that ensue can vary from personal caregiving tasks to financial and other responsibilities that are sometimes difficult to embrace – some things that families "just don't like to talk about." When this became so obvious in her own family, she recognized the need to get smart about the topic of caregiving from afar. This book reflects more than 10 years of collecting stories of acquaintances who have found themselves in the role of caregivers often without knowing how to get started or how to get better at supporting their loved ones who no longer knew how to stay safe and independent from a distance. Their stories are powerful testimonies about the variety of ways storytellers lovingly found to have peace of mind from afar.